D1105397

JUN

My name is Nate.

Nate and the horseshoe crabs

Words and illustrations by Nathaniel Newton

Hello, my name is Tern Tern!

Text and Illustrations © 2013 by Nathaniel Newton

First Edition

ISBN-10: 0615820034

Printed in USA

ISBN-13: 978-0-615-82003-3

Check out: natethepuffin.com

Library of Congress Control Number: 2013923119

Hi, my name is PJ!

Shhh...

Published by

Bookian®

Visit us at bookian.com

For the horseshoe crabs

On a bright moon spring night,
Nate is sound asleep dreaming
of fishing on beach with friends.

Nate wakes up eat breakfast
to start the day.

Nate's friends Tern Tern, PJ and Gully flew through his window to ask him to come out fishing on the beach.

Nate and his friends are flying along the beach when they notice thousands of horseshoe crabs covering the shoreline.

Nate said, "April through June, around the full moon, the Horseshoe crabs come out to play."

"We should help these horseshoe crabs get back to the ocean."

As Nate's friends get closer to the horseshoe crabs, they scream

"no way"!

"We are not touching these creepy critters because they can

sting us!"

Nate gently
turns the horseshoe crab
over and helps him get back on his feet.

"Horseshoe crabs do not sting,"

he told Tern Tern, PJ, and Gully. "They are
harmless creatures, who have been around since
before the dinosaurs."

They also provide many life saving
benefits for mankind."

Nate's friends still do not want to help the horseshoe crabs.

Nate said, "What if we were stuck on an island without wings to
fly home?"

Nate's friends imagine themselves
without wings on
an island and agree to help the
horseshoe crabs.

Nate and his friends
help all of the horseshoe crabs
get back to the ocean. Now they can
enjoy the delightful ocean blue they call home.

CPSIA information can be obtained
at www.ICGtesting.com
Printed in the USA
LVHW072100140519
617808LV00010B/409/P